PRAISE FOR
JASMINE TOGUCHI, MOCHI QUEEN

A JUNIOR LIBRARY GUILD SELECTION
AN AMAZON.COM BEST BOOK OF THE YEAR
A CHICAGO PUBLIC LIBRARY BEST OF THE BEST BOOKS

"In this new early chapter book series, Florence introduces readers to a bright character who is grappling with respecting authority while also forging her own path. Vuković's illustrations are expressive and imbue Jasmine and the Toguchi family with sweetness . . . **This first entry nicely balances humor with the challenges of growing up; readers will devour it.**"

—*School Library Journal*

"This first in the series handily introduces a plucky, **strong-willed girl whose family traditions may be new to many readers but whose frustrations will be familiar to nearly all.**"

—*The Horn Book*

"Adorable and heartwarming."

—*Booklist*

"Florence . . . warmly traces Jasmine's efforts to get strong (and fast), her clashes and tender moments with her family, and the ins and outs of making mochi . . . **[The] spot illustrations evoke Japanese Sumi-e painting while playfully capturing Jasmine's willfulness and her family's closeness.**"

—*Publishers Weekly*

"Florence paints **a lovely picture of a warm extended family** whose members truly care about one another and take each other seriously . . . **New readers thirsty for series fiction will look forward to more stories about Jasmine and her family.**"

—*Kirkus Reviews*

ENJOY MORE ADVENTURES WiTH
JASMINE TOGUCHI

Jasmine Toguchi, Mochi Queen

Jasmine Toguchi, Super Sleuth

Jasmine Toguchi, Drummer Girl

JASMINE TOGUCHI

FLAMINGO KEEPER

MINEGUCHI

FLAMINGO KEEPER

DEBBI MICHIKO FLORENCE PICTURES BY ELIZABET VUKOVIĆ

FARRAR STRAUS GIROUX • NEW YORK

Farrar Straus Giroux Books for Young Readers
An imprint of Macmillan Publishing Group, LLC
175 Fifth Avenue, New York, NY 10010

mackids.com

Library of Congress Cataloging-in-Publication Data

Names: Florence, Debbi Michiko, author. | Vuković, Elizabet, illustrator.
Title: Jasmine Toguchi, flamingo keeper / Debbi Michiko Florence ; pictures by
    Elizabet Vuković.
Description: First edition. | New York : Farrar Straus Giroux, 2018. |
    Series: Jasmine Toguchi | Summary: Jasmine makes a wish for a pet flamingo on
    the special daruma doll her grandmother sent from Japan, then sets out to prove
    herself responsible enough for a pet.
Identifiers: LCCN 2017042322 | ISBN 9780374304201 (hardcover) | ISBN
    9780374308377 (pbk.)
Subjects: | CYAC: Pets—Fiction. | Bodhidharma dolls—Fiction. | Dolls—Fiction. |
    Family life—Fiction. | Japanese Americans—Fiction.
Classification: LCC PZ7.1.F593 Jak 2018 | DDC [Fic]—dc23
LC record available at https://lccn.loc.gov/2017042322

Our books may be purchased in bulk for promotional, educational, or
business use. Please contact your local bookseller or the Macmillan
Corporate and Premium Sales Department at (800) 221-7945
ext. 5442 or by e-mail at MacmillanSpecialMarkets@macmillan.com.

IN MEMORY OF MY DAD, DENTA
HIROKANE, AND FOR MY MOM
AND STEPDAD, YASUKO AND
BOB FORDIANI, FOR PUTTING
UP WITH MY PARADE OF PETS
—D.M.F.

FOR ANA, MOJA BAKA—
GLIMPSES OF TIME
WITH YOU I'LL ALWAYS
REMEMBER —E.V.

CONTENTS

JASMINE TOGUCHI

FLAMINGO KEEPER

SATURDAY FUN DAY

I, Jasmine Toguchi, love Saturdays because Saturdays are super-fun days. Sometimes we have family time, when Dad, Mom, my sister, and I go to the zoo or the movies. Sometimes I play in my neighbor Mrs. Reese's garage. Today I get to have lunch with my best friend, Linnie Green, at her house.

"Jasmine, are you ready?" Mom called to me from the living room.

No, I was not ready. I was looking for my

special rock. Linnie collects rocks, and she gave me her favorite pink rock because it looks like a flamingo egg. Flamingos are my very favorite animal in the world. I wanted to bring the rock with me so she could see it again. I looked on my desk, but it wasn't there. I looked under my bed, but it wasn't there either.

"Why are you in your closet?" My big sister, Sophie, poked her head into my room. "If you don't get in the car right now, you're going to make me late for my soccer game."

"Walnuts! I can't find my rock," I said.

"Maybe you should check your head," Sophie said, and laughed. This was her way of joking, even if it wasn't very funny.

Ever since Sophie started fifth grade, she seemed to get bossier every day. Sophie was always telling me what I couldn't do. Like go into her room or touch her things. Sometimes I wondered if I had done something to make her mad at me. Or maybe she just didn't like me anymore. That made my chest feel tight and sad. But even having her say not-funny jokes to me was better than feeling invisible.

"Ha-ha," I said.

"Jasmine Toguchi," Mom shouted. "We're going to be late!"

"Hurry up!" Sophie said.

I took one last look around my bedroom and then ran after my sister. My flamingo-egg rock would have to stay behind.

★ ★ ★

"You're here!" Linnie shouted as she flung open her front door.

I turned to wave at my parents, and they drove off to take Sophie to her soccer game. I followed Linnie into her house.

There was a little blanket in the middle of the living room. That was different. Linnie is very neat and never leaves things lying around. Then we walked through to the kitchen.

"What's that?" I asked, pointing to a bowl of water on the floor. Mrs. Green is also very neat. She doesn't even leave her cooking things out on the counter, so it was strange she would

leave something
on the floor.

"A surprise,"
Linnie said, giggling.

I like a good surprise, but I wasn't sure about this one. What if the surprise was that we were going to clean up? Or maybe eat lunch on the floor? Actually, that might not be so bad. It could be fun, like a picnic. I hoped the surprise was a picnic and not cleaning. I am *not* a fan of cleaning.

I have been to Linnie's house a million times, so it feels like a second home to me. I walked down the hall to her bedroom because that's what we always do. We always go to her room for her special suitcase that's filled with a bunch of old Halloween costumes. We play dress up and pretend we are princesses, ballerinas, knights, and bunnies. But Linnie didn't follow me.

"Where are you?" I called out.

"Over here," she said, laughing. "Come this way!"

Linnie stood at the sliding glass door to the backyard. This surprised me, since Linnie doesn't like playing outside. She is afraid of dirt and heights and bugs. Okay, maybe not *afraid*. But she doesn't like those things as much as I do. Linnie is trying to be braver these days. Maybe this was her surprise, that we were going to play outside!

Linnie held a tennis ball. Were we going to

play catch? I didn't really *love* to play catch. It was boring throwing a ball back and forth, but because Linnie is my very best friend in the world, I am happy to do things that she likes to do.

Linnie opened the sliding door, and I followed her into the yard. And that's when I heard a strange sound.

LINNIE'S SURPRISE

"Woof!"

Before I could ask Linnie what that sound was, a little black-and-white dog galloped toward us.

"Wowee zowee, Linnie!" I said. "Is that a puppy?"

Linnie sat down, and the dog scrambled over and licked Linnie's face. "Sure is," she said. "And she's *my* puppy! Her name is Trixie."

I sat down next to Linnie on the grass and

the puppy leaped into my lap and started licking my face, too. It tickled and I laughed. But I closed my lips quickly, because as much as I liked dog kisses, I did *not* want dog slobber in my mouth!

Linnie threw the ball across the yard. Trixie ran after it.

"My parents finally got me a dog," Linnie said with a huge smile. "I've been asking for one for a long time!"

"You're so lucky," I said.

Trixie bounded back over with the ball in her mouth. Linnie took the ball and threw it

for her puppy again. Now I knew why there was a bowl on the kitchen floor and a blanket in the living room. They were for Trixie.

As we played fetch, the ball got wetter and wetter with dog slobber, but I didn't mind. I just wiped it off onto my jean shorts.

"Trixie is so cute with her black spot and waggy tail," I said. "How did you convince your parents to get you a dog?" Maybe I could try some of Linnie's tricks to convince *my* parents to get me a pet flamingo, even though Mom says flamingos belong in the wild.

"I had to show my mom and dad that I was responsible enough to take care of a pet," Linnie said. "That means I had to take care of myself without being told, like keeping my room clean, brushing my teeth, and clearing the table after meals."

That sounded like a lot of work.

"I also showed them how much I knew about taking care of a dog, like feeding it and taking it for walks. I read a lot of books about dogs."

I liked to read.

"The truth is," Linnie said with a smile, "my mom really wanted a dog, too, so it didn't take a lot of convincing."

I was pretty sure I was the only one in my family who wanted a pet flamingo. I would have to work hard to make my parents believe I would be a good flamingo keeper.

* * *

Mom picked me up after lunch.

"Linnie got a puppy named Trixie!" I told her. "She is so soft and fluffy. We played fetch and then we walked her around the block on her leash. Then I got to feed Trixie some dog cookies. She loved those! Linnie is going to teach her tricks like roll over and sit up!"

"It sounds like you two had a lot of fun," Mom said. "I'll bet Linnie's very happy with her new puppy."

"She is," I said. And soon I'd be very happy with my own pet flamingo. I just wasn't sure how to go about getting one yet.

When we pulled into our driveway, Sophie was waiting for us. That was strange. She had changed out of her soccer uniform and into her regular clothes. That was not so strange. As soon as Mom stopped the car and turned off the engine, Sophie ran over to Mom's side and opened her door. That was strange.

Mom must have thought so, too, because when she got out of the car she asked, "Is something wrong?"

"Quick!" Sophie said, and started pulling on Mom's arm.

"What's going on?" Mom asked, tripping as Sophie tugged her toward the house.

I ran after Mom and Sophie. Had Sophie broken something in the house? No, if she had, she wouldn't rush to show Mom. Was Dad hurt? A tickle of worry wiggled its way through me, making my stomach feel funny. I caught up to them just as they walked through the back door into the kitchen.

SPECIAL DELIVERY

Sophie dashed to the kitchen table and pointed to two small boxes wrapped in brown paper. "Dad said I had to wait till you and Jasmine got home."

Mom put her hand to her heart. "You scared me, Sophie! I thought something was wrong."

"Can I open mine now?" Sophie picked up one of the packages.

"What is it?" I asked. I scooted around the

table and peeked at the other box. "This one has my name on it!"

"Who sent them?" Mom asked.

"Obaachan!" I said, reading the return address from Hiroshima, Japan.

"Why is your grandma sending you packages?" Mom smiled. "It's not your birthdays or Christmas."

"It must be *just because*," I said.

Sometimes we got *just because* presents. Just because Sophie and I behaved well at the store, or just because Mom or Dad saw something we'd like, or just because they love us. They were usually fun little gifts. Once, Mom got me an eraser shaped like a flamingo. Sophie got one shaped like a soccer ball.

"Moooooom, please can we open them?" Sophie waved the box in Mom's face.

Mom laughed. "Yes, you both may open your packages. Together."

Dad walked in as Sophie and I sat at the

table. Sophie tore the paper off her package, tossing bits and pieces to the floor.

"Sophie Toguchi," Mom said. That was a change. Usually Mom said *my* full name like that.

I liked to savor a surprise. On her birthday, Sophie always tore through her gifts. But I took my time opening each present.

"Sophie, wait till your sister unwraps hers before you open the box."

"Jasmine!" Sophie said. "Hurry!"

Instead of hurrying, I moved super-slowly. Everyone was always telling me what to do. Mom. Dad. Sophie. I carefully peeled back the tape from the brown paper.

"What's taking you so long?" Sophie asked.

"I want to save these," I said. I was going to cut out the stamps from Japan and put them in a collage.

I shot a grin at my sister. But Sophie was giving me such a glare, it felt like a laser sizzling right through my brain.

"I'm going to open my box," Sophie announced.

Dad chuckled. "Patience, Sophie."

I sped up, partly because I didn't want Sophie to be mad at me and mostly because I wanted to see what Obaachan had sent us. I slid off the brown wrapping paper and gripped the white cardboard box. Knowing Obaachan, she got me and Sophie the same thing, whatever it was. I didn't want Sophie to know before I did.

"On three, okay?" Sophie said to me as she grasped her box. "One. Two. Three!"

We both lifted the lids at the same time.

I peeked into my box. It was something rounded and red. Maybe Obaachan got me a ball? That didn't feel very special. My heart sank to my toes, but I tried not to show my disappointment. That would be ungrateful, and Mom has a rule that we have to be gracious when receiving gifts.

"What is this?" Sophie asked.

I reached into my box and pulled out a whatever-it-was. It was light like a ball, but not round like a ball. It felt like it was made from thick paper or cardboard. It was oval-shaped with a flat bottom.

"It looks like a doll," I said, thinking Obaachan prob-ably didn't know that Sophie had stopped play-ing with dolls.

"It has no eyeballs!" Sophie screeched, and she threw the doll-thing in the air.

MAKE A WISH

Sophie's doll-thing flew through the kitchen. Dad caught it.

"Oh," he said. "It's a daruma!"

"What's that?" I was much braver than Sophie. I wasn't afraid of a strange-looking present. I peered at the odd thing in my hand. It had a peach-colored face with black eyebrows and a beard. A boy doll, then. He had a red slash for a mouth. Not quite happy, but not quite mad either. Gold lines radiated out around his face. The strangest thing was that the doll had blank white circles instead of eyes.

"It's a wishing doll," Mom said. "You make a wish and color in one eye. When the wish is fulfilled, you color in the other eye."

"Wowee zowee!" I said. "That's super-cool!"

"I think you mean super-*creepy*," Sophie said. She stood behind her chair, looking like she wanted to run away. Even though she didn't play with dolls anymore, this one seemed different, not so much for playing with.

"Are these only for kids?" I asked, glancing at Sophie.

Dad gave me a smile like he knew what I was up to. "No, Jasmine. Even adults like daruma. In fact, I had one in college."

"Obaachan used to give me one every year when I was a teenager," Mom said.

Sophie reached for her daruma, and Dad handed it back to her.

"What did you wish for?" I asked my parents. "And did you get to color in both eyes?"

"I can't remember all of mine," Mom said. "But I think I eventually colored in all the eyes. Some wishes took longer to come true."

"Like what?" Sophie asked.

"Once, I wished for a dictionary," Mom said. "I got one for my next birthday. Another time, in high school, I wished to be the editor of the school newspaper. That took two years, but I became the editor in my senior year."

"Oh," I said. "It has to be a serious wish?" That didn't sound like much fun. I didn't want to wish for good grades or anything like that.

Dad patted my shoulder. "Wish for whatever you want. Just know that some wishes can take a while to get."

"What did you wish for?" I asked Dad.

He flashed a grin at Mom. "I wished that the prettiest and smartest woman in college would go out with me."

"Oh, brother." Sophie groaned.

"And she said yes when I asked her out." Dad smiled at Mom again. "My wish came true very quickly."

Okay, so it didn't have to be a serious wish about school or work. Good.

"I know what I'm going to wish for," Sophie said.

"What?" I asked.

"I'm not telling." Sophie put her doll on the table and rummaged through the pen drawer for a black marker.

"Are you not supposed to tell?" I asked Mom and Dad.

Dad shrugged. "I don't think there are any hard-and-fast rules."

I looked at Mom because she was the one with all the rules. If there was a rule, she would know it. She shook her head. "If you want to tell, you can, Jasmine. But you don't have to."

"I'm not going to tell," Sophie said.

"You said that already," I replied, and Sophie made a face at me.

My sister uncapped her marker and sat down at the table. She stared at her daruma. I hoped she would whisper her wish to her doll so I could hear it. No such luck. After a minute, Sophie picked up the daruma and drew a round eyeball in one of the blank circles on her doll's face. When she capped her marker, she waved it at me, but I shook my head. I wasn't ready to color in my doll's eye. There were so many things I could wish for.

"I'm going to put this right next to my bed." Sophie smiled at her doll, which she carefully held in her hands.

I followed Sophie down the hall. "What did you wish?" I asked.

"I said, I'm not telling!"

"Did you wish for a good grade on a test? Or maybe a new soccer ball? Did you wish for something like a birthday party at Disneyland?" I asked. "Or maybe dinner at a fancy restaurant?"

"Stop following me." Sophie faced me when she got to her room.

"Mom and Dad said it was okay to tell your wish," I said.

"I know, but I don't want to tell *you*. Now go away."

Sophie closed the door on me. I stood there blinking. I didn't know why she was so mean to me. It wasn't like I'd make fun of her wish or tell anyone if she wanted to keep it a secret. I crossed my arms. She didn't want to tell me her wish? Fine! I wouldn't tell her mine!

But first I needed to figure out the best wish ever. It didn't matter if I didn't know Sophie's wish. *My* wish was going to be better and bigger and more special than anything she could wish for. This was going to take some serious thinking. I knew just where to go.

THINKING TREE

After I told Mom and Dad where I was going, I ran to Mrs. Reese's house. Mrs. Reese is our neighbor two houses away. She's my friend even though she's older than Mom and Dad. She bakes me brownies without nuts, lets me play in her garage, and says it's okay for me to climb the apricot tree in her backyard. It's my special thinking spot.

I scrambled over Mrs. Reese's gate and ran to my tree. The branches waved in the breeze like the tree was greeting me.

"Hello, Tree," I said.

"Hello, Jasmine." It was not the tree that answered, because that would be silly. Trees can't talk. It was Mrs. Reese.

I turned around. Mrs. Reese sat on a chair, reading. Usually she sat on her front porch to read, but today was especially hot and sunny. Her backyard had more shade.

"Do you need to do some thinking this afternoon?" Mrs. Reese asked.

"Yes."

"Go ahead, then," she said. "I won't bother you."

That's another thing I like about Mrs. Reese. She lets me do my thing without lecturing me or giving me a bunch of rules.

I climbed the tree up to my favorite spot, in

the crook of a branch. I could sit with my back against the trunk and think. I stared at the leaves. What should I wish for? There was a whole wide world of possibilities. How would I be able to choose just *one* thing? I grinned so hard my cheeks hurt. This was very exciting!

I loved chocolate. I could wish for a lifetime supply of chocolate. Or I could wish for Mrs. Reese to bake me brownies without nuts every week. I rubbed my tummy. Then again, maybe that would be too much chocolate. Was there such a thing?

I could wish for books. Or for a new

babysitter. I sure would have liked to have a babysitter who was fun and nice instead of boring Mrs. Peepers. I could wish that Sophie liked me again. That would be a great wish, but that might take a long time to come true. I wanted to color in the other eye of my daruma fast. Thinking of only one wish was hard!

Maybe I should wish to find my flamingo-egg rock. Although Linnie didn't seem to miss it, especially now that she had her very own pet.

Oh! That's what I could wish for. My very own pet! Not just any pet, but my very own *flamingo*! Once I had it, Mom would see what a great pet a flamingo could be. I was so happy I felt like I would float into the sky.

I shimmied down the tree and hopped over to Mrs. Reese. When I'm full of energy and excitement, I like to hop. I hopped twice on my left foot, twice on my right, and then for fun, I jumped up and down three times.

"That must be some great idea you have there, Jasmine," Mrs. Reese said with a smile.

"It is! Thank you for letting me use your tree!"

"Anytime," Mrs. Reese said.

I ran all the way home. Dad was mowing the front yard and he waved to me as I zoomed past him into the house. I grabbed my daruma from the kitchen table. I ran past Mom, who was needlepointing in the living room. When I got to my room, I set the daruma on my desk. I opened my drawer full of markers. I had every color of the rainbow for my collages.

I dug around in the drawer and my fingers hit something that did not feel like a marker. It was the flamingo-egg rock! I must have put it in my drawer when I was cleaning up. Sometimes I rush when I clean up, especially if Mom tells me I can't do something I want to do until my room is clean. Good thing I didn't waste my wish on finding the rock!

I put the pink rock next to my daruma. "I think you're good luck," I said to the doll. How perfect that I found my flamingo-egg rock at the same time I was about to make my special wish!

I chose a purple marker because purple is my favorite color. I uncapped the marker and carefully colored in an eye with purple. When

I was done, I picked up the doll to check it out. Perfect!

I held him up and said out loud, "I wish I could have a pet flamingo." And then I kissed the top of his head for extra luck.

PET STORE

On Sunday, Linnie invited me to go with her and Mrs. Green to the pet store. Linnie was planning to use her allowance to buy a toy for Trixie.

The pet store smelled like pine shavings. The first area we passed was the fish section. I stood in front of a large tank filled with fish.

"So many goldfish!" Linnie said. "And so many colors!"

"Look over here," I said. "The sign says these

are called angelfish, but they don't really look like angels."

I watched the fish for a few seconds longer. They seemed like they were flying through the water—so graceful, like when my friend Daisy Wang dances ballet.

After the fish, Linnie and I wandered over to the bunnies and guinea pigs. Then we walked all the way to the back where the birds were. They had parakeets, canaries, finches, and a parrot. I loved watching the birds.

"Guess what?" I said to Linnie as she chirped to a lovebird.

"What?"

"I got a special wishing doll from Obaachan and I wished for a pet flamingo," I said with a grin.

"Awesome!" Linnie said. "How do you get a flamingo? Will it come in the mail, or does it fly to you? I wonder when it will happen. Oh!

Maybe you should get a toy for your new pet today, too! I'm so excited for you!"

Linnie grabbed my hand and pulled me over to the dog section.

I thought about what Linnie had said. How *would* the flamingo get to my house? Was the daruma like Santa Claus, and he would bring the flamingo to me down the chimney? Or was it magical like wishing on birthday candles? Maybe the flamingo would just *POOF* appear in the living room one day soon. Tomorrow, I hoped!

While Linnie looked at the dog toys, I wandered down the aisle. When Linnie and I took Trixie for a walk yesterday, Trixie had pulled and tugged us all over the place. Sometimes Trixie sat down and refused to move. I wondered if my flamingo would need a leash. Our neighbors probably wouldn't appreciate having a flamingo running through their yards. I stopped and stared up at the collars. Flamingos had really skinny necks. Would there be a collar small enough?

"What are you looking for?" Mrs. Green asked me.

"A flamingo collar," I said, pointing to the top row.

Mrs. Green reached up for a little purple

collar. Because she is the mom of my very best friend, she knows that my favorite color is purple and that I love flamingos. I held the collar and squinted at it. I slipped it onto my wrist.

"How skinny is a flamingo's neck?" Mrs. Green asked. Good question.

"I don't really know," I said. Come to think of it, I didn't know a whole lot about flamingos, but I loved watching them. We saw them every time we went to the zoo. I loved how they strutted around like they were proud of their bright pink feathers. They made a lot of great sounds, too. Muttering, but also calling out in loud honks. But I didn't know what they ate or liked to do. If I was going to be a good flamingo keeper, I would need to know those things. I handed the collar back to Mrs. Green. I realized I should do some research before I bought anything for my new pet.

Linnie danced up to us with a stuffed squirrel.

Mrs. Green laughed. "Yes, Trixie does seem to want to catch a squirrel."

"Trixie chases them through the yard, but she isn't fast enough. This one," Linnie explained, holding up the stuffed toy, "Trixie will be able to catch, at least."

In line at the register, a family ahead of us was buying a rabbit. The boy was very happy about his new pet. I was getting excited about *my* soon-to-be new pet! I had no idea how or when it would appear, but I knew I'd better figure out how to take care of it before then.

A PROJECT

Bong bong bong bing!

On Monday morning, Ms. Sanchez, my third-grade teacher, played the start-of-the-day song on her xylophone. Everyone in room 5 sat up straight and got quiet.

"Buenos días!" Ms. Sanchez said. "I have a special announcement. This week we are going to do a fun project. You will each get a chance to be a teacher."

That sounded exciting! I imagined standing

at the front of the room, playing Ms. Sanchez's xylophone to get class started. I would make reading time longer.

"You each will pick something you want to learn about," Ms. Sanchez said. "We'll go to the library and you'll find a book about your topic. You'll read the book, and then you will do an oral report to teach the rest of the class about it."

Hmmm. That didn't sound as fun as I had imagined, but then I got an idea. I would learn all about flamingos so I would know how to take care of mine when I got it. Then the next time I went to the pet store, I would know what to buy. Mom would be impressed with my flamingo knowledge and then she'd be happy to let me keep my pet!

A few minutes later, room 5 lined up and we followed Ms. Sanchez down the hall to the library. It is like a big bookstore, but everything is free. I borrow books, read them, and then return them to the library and get even more books. It's the best!

When we got there, Ms. Groff, the librarian, greeted us as we sat down. Ms. Groff has curly hair and is very tall, probably so she can reach books on the higher shelves.

"Good morning, room 5," Ms. Groff said. "Remember, when you go to the computer to look up your topic, find the call number for the

subject and write it down. Then use the call number to find the section in the library where your book is. Once you get your books, bring them to me so I can help you check them out. Have fun looking for your books and if you need help, you can ask me or Ms. Sanchez."

"What are you going to learn about?" I asked Linnie.

"I think I will read about training puppies," she said.

"How about the rest of you?" I asked my friends as we stood up to look for our books.

"I already know about a lot of things," Maggie Milsap said. Maggie was a know-it-all, but I was getting used to her. She moved here to Los Angeles from Portland, Oregon, at the start of the school year. Now we are friends, kind of. "It's going to be hard for me to find something I don't know much about," she said.

Tommy rolled his eyes. He had the least

patience for Maggie, but he tried to be nice, too. "I'm going to learn about karate."

Tommy said it the Japanese way: *kah-rah-teh*. I don't speak Japanese like my parents, but I know some words. And I know how to pronounce them the right way.

"I didn't know you liked karate," I said.

"My cousin started taking lessons and it looks fun," Tommy said.

We all turned to Daisy Wang. She was already very good at ballet dancing. Her mom is a baker and makes the most delicious treats, which Daisy always shares with us. "I will read about sunflowers. I want to grow them in our garden this summer."

"What are you going to do your report on?" Tommy asked me.

"I know, I know," Linnie said, smiling. "Flamingos!"

There was only one book on flamingos at our library. I copied down the call number and went to look for it.

After Linnie, Tommy, Daisy, and I found our books, we helped Maggie.

"How about this?" I asked, holding up a book about cats.

"I'm allergic," she said.

"Since you're from Oregon but live here now," Linnie said, "maybe you can learn about California."

Maggie shook her head. "Oregon is the best

state in the world. I don't need to learn about California."

"Chocolate?" Daisy asked, holding up a book. "Everyone loves chocolate."

"Sweets aren't good for you. They rot your teeth." Maggie's mom is a dentist.

"Okay, class," Ms. Sanchez announced. "Five more minutes. If you haven't checked out your book yet, now is the time to see Ms. Groff."

"Help!" Maggie said to us.

"They're trying," Tommy said.

Maggie sniffed. "Fine! I'll close my eyes and pick a book. It doesn't really matter anyway."

Maggie reached onto a shelf and pulled out a book. We crowded around her to see what it was. Tommy started laughing.

"*Things That Explode.*" I read the title for everyone.

Maggie scrunched her face at Tommy. "Why are you laughing? This is a fascinating topic! I'll become an expert. Just you wait!"

I took my pretty book about flamingos to Ms. Groff, who scanned it into the computer and handed it back to me.

"I hope you enjoy your book," she said.

I definitely would! Maybe my flamingo would be waiting for me at the house today. I'd better get reading!

RESEARCH

When I got home after school, I looked in the backyard to see if my flamingo was there. Nope. I ran into the house and checked the fireplace. Nothing. I peered up into the chimney. I hoped he wasn't stuck or something. I searched my bedroom, the bathroom, and even the closet. No flamingo. Maybe it wasn't time yet. Maybe the daruma was waiting to make sure I would know how to take care of my pet.

I went back to my room with my book. For homework, Ms. Sanchez had told us to start reading the books we'd checked out.

I set my daruma right in front of me so he could watch me learning about flamingos. I flipped through the pages to look at the photographs. On the first page was a picture of a group of pink flamingos with black-tipped beaks and long skinny legs. Just looking at them made me happy. I turned the page. Baby flamingos are gray. I didn't know that. On the next page was a picture of flamingos flying!

After I looked at the
pictures, I started to read.
There is more than one
type of flamingo. The
biggest one is called the
greater flamingo. That's

the one I wanted! They need to be near calm,
salty water, like certain types of lakes. They
hang their heads upside down to eat, swishing
their beaks to catch little shrimpy things.
Their food is what gives them pink feathers!

Wowee zowee!

I didn't know where
the closest salty lake
was to our house. Tommy
Fraser has a swimming
pool in his backyard.
Maybe he would let me
fill it with salt water for
my flamingo. I would
teach my flamingo to

play fetch like Linnie plays with Trixie. I could throw a shrimp toy for him. I imagined my flamingo flying across my yard to chase his toy. I smiled and hugged myself.

I took out a piece of paper and started making a list of things I would need for my pet flamingo, like a Frisbee for fetch. I didn't know where to get the shrimpy things they ate, but I knew the Japanese market sold

yummy shrimp chips. I added that to my list. I worked hard until Mom called me for dinner.

When I sat down to dinner, I cheered. We were having not only roast chicken and mashed potatoes, but also edamame, my favorite vegetable. It's my favorite because it's fun to eat! Edamame are soybeans that you pop from the pod into your mouth. One time, back when Sophie used to play with me, we had an edamame war. We popped the beans at each other during dinner. Mom didn't like that at all. Now we have a rule that edamame can only be popped onto your plate or into your mouth.

As I ate my dinner, I thought about my list of things I needed for my flamingo.

"Dad?" I asked. "Can you build a lake in our backyard?" It would be easier to have my own lake than to have to take my pet to Tommy's house.

"Why do you want a lake in our backyard?" Dad asked.

I didn't want to say anything about my wish at dinner. Mostly because Sophie hadn't told me hers, so I didn't want her to know mine. Plus, a small part of me worried that Mom and Dad wouldn't let me keep a pet. Better to wait until my flamingo was here.

"I'm just asking if you could do it," I said. "You know, since you're so good at building things."

Dad smiled. "Well, I suppose if I put my mind to it, I could build a lake."

"That's good to know," I said.

"What are you up to?" Sophie asked.

"I'm not telling you," I said.

"Whatever." Sophie went back to eating her chicken.

After dinner, Sophie came into my room. I wasn't allowed to go into her room without asking first, but I was happy to have her in mine.

She picked up my daruma. "What did you wish for?" she asked.

"What did *you* wish for?" I asked.

Sophie flipped her hair over her shoulder and stared at me, not in a mean way, though. "I'll tell you soon. First, tell me your wish."

"You'll tell me? Promise?"

"Yes, eventually. Just not yet."

"Why can't you tell me now?"

"I want to keep it to myself a little longer," she said. "Once I share it, it will become everyone else's wish, too."

Interesting. But I had liked sharing my wish with Linnie. She was happy and excited for

me. I wanted to
share it with my
sister, too.

"I wished for a
pet flamingo," I
said.

"You can't keep
a flamingo for a
pet," Sophie said.

"Mom and Dad would never let you."

I nibbled my bottom lip. I suddenly understood why Sophie might not want to share her
wish after all. "It's my wish," I said. "They
can't stop it from happening."

"Good luck with that," Sophie said, leaving
my room.

I didn't need luck. I had my daruma wish. I
opened my flamingo book again and looked at
a picture of a bunch of flamingos together. I
read the words under the picture. Flamingos
liked to live in a big group, or flock. *Walnuts!*

I wondered if Mom and Dad would let me get more than one. I didn't want my flamingo to be lonesome.

I patted my daruma. I hoped he knew what he was doing. "Please make my wish come true soon," I whispered.

OBAACHAN'S LESSON

"Girls," Mom called to me and Sophie from her office.

When I got there, she had the computer turned on.

"Let's call Obaachan so you can thank her for the gifts," Mom said, opening the video-chat program.

"But it's nighttime," I said. Whenever Obaachan stayed with us, she liked to go to bed early and read. Sometimes she went to bed at the same time as I did, and I had an early bedtime.

"Remember, in Japan they are sixteen hours ahead of our time," Mom explained.

"So it's morning there now," Sophie said.

I counted in my head. It was seven o'clock here, so that meant it was eleven o'clock in the morning there.

Sophie and I jostled in the one chair in front of the computer. Mom sighed and pushed

two chairs together and made us each sit in our own chair.

"Ohayo gozai masu," Mom said when Obaachan appeared on the screen.

It was weird to hear Mom say good morning when it was night for us.

"Konbanwa." Obaachan said good evening to us.

Sophie and I tried to wait patiently while Mom and Obaachan spoke to each other in Japanese. Finally, Mom stepped away and nodded to us.

"Domo arigato for the daruma," I said.

"Yeah, thank you very much," Sophie said.

"You make wish?" Obaachan asked.

"Hai!" Sophie and I said yes at the same time.

"You work hard, gambatte," Obaachan said.

"What's *gambatte*?" Sophie asked.

"It mean you no give up. You work hard, make wish come true," Obaachan said. She lifted a daruma with both eyes colored in. "The face, it serious. He remind you, gambatte."

I frowned. "Wait a minute. You have to make your own wish come true?" I *knew* there would be rules. There were always rules.

"Yes," Obaachan said. "Nothing come free. You work hard. You make goal."

Sophie glanced at me. "That means whatever we wished for doesn't magically happen?" Sophie asked.

Obaachan looked confused. She doesn't know a lot of English. Mom stepped in and translated and Obaachan nodded.

"Right. No magic. Hard work. No give up," Obaachan said.

Sophie looked at me again, but I ignored her.

After we said goodbye to Obaachan, I brushed my teeth and changed into my pajamas. I crawled into bed and faced my wall where I had a collage of flamingos hanging. I reached out and traced a long neck, long legs, and pink wings. If what Obaachan said was right, that meant a flamingo wouldn't magically appear anytime soon. And there was no way my parents would just give me a flamingo if I asked for it. What was the point of a wish if I had to work to make it come true?

I flipped onto my back and stared out my window at the darkening sky. I liked to leave my shades up so I could see the stars and the moon.

I thought about other wishes I'd made. At New Year's, I wished I could pound mochi with the men even though the family rules said I couldn't. But I made my arm muscles strong to convince my family that I could pound mochi. And I did it! For our school talent show, I wished to have a great talent to show off and I learned how to play the taiko drum. Maybe I could make my flamingo wish come true, too!

I was already learning about how to take care of a flamingo. That was a good first step.

Linnie had to prove to her parents that she was responsible enough to keep a pet. That's what I would do next. I would show Mom and Dad I was super-responsible. Then they would get me a pet flamingo! I smiled as my eyes fluttered closed. I had a plan.

ACTION!

On Tuesday, when I got home from school, I went straight to my room and did my homework.

"Mom, look!" I ran into the kitchen, where Mom was working. She raised her finger and I waited while she finished writing. Mom is an editor. She works with writers and fixes their mistakes, kind of like a teacher.

Mom capped her blue pen and turned to me. "What's up, Jasmine?" she asked with a smile.

"I finished all my homework," I said, showing her my math paper. "And you didn't even need to remind me."

"Good job, Jasmine."

"I'm going to clean my room now," I said.

Mom wrinkled her forehead. "Why?" she asked.

"Don't you want me to clean my room?"

"Of course, but usually I have to tell you over and over."

"I guess I'm becoming more responsible," I said.

"I guess you are."

I ran to my room to clean up. It was a lot of work to be responsible, but it would be worth it when I got my own flamingo.

As I cleaned, I wondered where we would get my pet. The pet store didn't have flamingos for sure. Maybe I could order one online.

I grabbed my flamingo library book out of my backpack. I'd already read it three times.

In class, Ms. Sanchez had taught us how to take notes, so I had pages of fun facts. I knew a lot about flamingos now, like that they build nests out of mud and they have webbed feet. But maybe I missed the part about where to buy a flamingo. I read the book again, but nowhere did it say how to get a flamingo of my own.

The only place I'd ever seen flamingos was at the zoo. Did the zoo sell their animals like a pet store did? I would have to research that. But first I needed to show my parents that I'd be a responsible flamingo keeper.

On Wednesday morning, I helped Dad take the trash out.

"Wow, you're being a great helper," Dad said as he picked up bits of trash behind me. "Why don't you let me carry that bag while you hold this garbage can?"

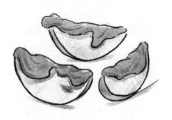

On Wednesday after school, I helped Mom make our snacks.

"Thanks, Jasmine," Mom said, wiping the counter. "Why don't you let me spread the peanut butter on the apples while you get the napkins?"

At dinner, whenever anyone asked for something like the soy sauce or the pepper, I made sure I was the one to pass it.

"Jasmine Toguchi," Mom said. "Please don't lunge across the table like that."

On Thursday, I didn't have to work so

hard at being responsible, since it was only Mrs. Peepers, our boring babysitter, and Sophie after school.

"When are you going to tell me your wish?" I asked Sophie as we walked to our rooms for reading time. Mrs. Peepers made sure we did our homework quietly at the kitchen table. Then, if we were good, we got to read in our rooms until Mom came home.

"Soon. Now that I know my wish isn't going to magically come true, I need to figure out how to make it happen," Sophie said. "What are you going to do about your wish?"

"I'm working on it," I said. I hopped twice on my left foot and twice on my right. I was excited. "I'm sure my wish will come true very soon."

"Really?" Sophie said. She didn't seem to believe me, but I didn't care. She was probably jealous that I was going to have a pet and she wasn't!

I went into my room and straightened up my desk so it would be neat by the time Mom got home. I patted my daruma on his head. With all my responsibility, Mom and Dad would get me a flamingo for sure!

THE BiG DAY

Friday was the big day. I was going to ask Mom and Dad to help make my wish come true. I'd been responsible all week, and I got the highest mark possible on my oral report on flamingos. I was ready for my pet!

It was pizza night for dinner. Every few weeks we got to make our own pizzas. Dad bought fresh dough on his way home from work and Mom chopped up all kinds of ingredients, like mushrooms (blech), olives (yum), onions (meh), and more. I put cheese and pepperoni on mine.

"Guess what?" I said as soon as we all sat down.

"What?" Mom said.

"I got a 4 on my oral report on flamingos today!" I sat up straight. "Ms. Sanchez liked that I did extra work by doing a flamingo collage with facts. She called me a flamingo expert!"

"That's fantastic, Jasmine," Dad said. "I'm proud of you!"

"I know so much about flamingos that I'd make a great flamingo keeper," I said.

"Maybe you can work at the zoo someday," Mom said.

I frowned. That was not the answer I was hoping for.

"Don't you think I could take care of a flamingo now?" I asked.

Mom tilted her head at me.

"Jasmine wants a pet flamingo," Sophie said.

"Sophie!" She'd ruined my moment.

"What?" Sophie tossed her hair over her shoulder.

"Oh, Jasmine," Mom said. "I'm afraid that's not possible."

"Why not?" I said, louder than I meant to. "I am very responsible! I did *all* my homework without you reminding me. I kept my room clean this week. I helped Dad take out the trash."

Mom reached out to pat my arm, but I pulled my arm into my lap, away from her.

"Sweetie," Dad said. "Flamingos are wild animals, not pets. If you love flamingos as much as you say you do, you'd want them to be happy, right? A flamingo would not be happy living at our house."

I thought about how the book said flamingos like to live in flocks. I thought about how flamingos need salty water and those shrimpy things to eat in order to stay pink. I slumped in my seat.

"Jasmine Toguchi," Mom said. "Please don't put your head on the table. You'll get cheese in your hair."

I lifted my heavy head. "Can I please be excused?"

"You didn't eat your dinner," Mom said.

"Sophie can have mine," I said. I wasn't hungry anymore.

As I walked to my room, I heard Sophie say, "Jasmine wished for a pet flamingo for her daruma wish."

"Oh dear," Mom said.

✳ ✳ ✳

Mom and Dad came to my room after they were done with dinner. Mom put a plate of sliced apples and bananas for me on my nightstand.

"I'm sorry you're disappointed, Jasmine," Mom said, sitting next to me on my bed.

Dad sat down on my other side and put his arm around me. "You're allowed to feel sad. I hope you'll realize that this is best for everyone. It would have been very hard to keep a flamingo in our house. Can you imagine the mess it would make?"

I looked up at Dad, who was smiling.

"Flamingos have long necks," Mom said. "He would probably knock over our books and pictures on the shelves in the living room."

I squinted at Mom.

"And I'll bet flamingos are hard to housebreak," Dad added. "There would be flamingo poop all over the floor." He waggled his eyebrows at me, almost making me smile.

"Probably there would be feathers everywhere," I said, getting the hang of it. "On the couch, in the bathtub, and in our food."

"Yes," Mom said. "We'd be sneezing from the feathers."

I smiled a small smile imagining my family sneezing all the time.

"I would need to make a lake in the backyard, but we have a water shortage in California," Dad reminded me.

I nodded. "Right. Plus, we like to use our backyard. We wouldn't have room to play anymore."

"Or have picnics," Mom said, patting my hand.

"I learned that flamingos need to live with other flamingos in a flock," I said.

"Oh," Mom said. "Then we'd need even more room and we don't have a very big backyard."

I sighed. My nose tingled and my heart felt sad. I glanced out my window into the yard, the yard where my pet flamingo would never play fetch with me. I looked down at my bedroom floor, the floor where my pet flamingo would never sleep near me. I wasn't going to get a flamingo. Not today, not ever. It wasn't fair. My biggest wish in the world would never come true.

"But we can visit them at the zoo," Mom said.

I nodded, because I knew Mom and Dad were trying to cheer me up, but I couldn't help the fat tears that rolled down my face.

Mom and Dad both wrapped their arms around me and hugged me as I cried.

SOPHIE'S WISH

When I woke up on Saturday morning, I rolled over and rubbed my eyes. They felt puffy from crying.

The daruma was on my desk. Even though Mom and Dad had tried to cheer me up, it didn't change the fact that I could never color in my daruma's other eye. He would have only one eye forever. This was a huge dilemma.

I climbed out of bed and sat at my desk. Sometimes when I'm sad, I make a collage and it helps me feel better. I would make a collage of dogs for Linnie.

I cut out a picture of a black-and-white puppy from one of Mom's magazines. She gives me her magazines after she finishes reading them. Then I snip out whatever pictures and words I like.

Sophie walked into my room and stood next to my desk. "You missed breakfast," she said.

I'd eaten the fruit Mom left for me before I went to bed last night. I still wasn't very hungry because my stomach was full of sadness. I put down my scissors and got my glue stick.

"Mom said to let you sleep in," Sophie said. She reached over and picked up my daruma. "I went on an errand with Dad."

Sophie was bragging about hanging out with Dad. She had promised to tell me her wish, but she hadn't. I didn't feel like talking to Sophie. "Don't you have somewhere else to be?" I asked as I carefully glued the black-and-white puppy picture in the center of the collage. I always put the most important picture in the middle.

Sophie huffed out a breath like she was annoyed. "Come with me," she said.

Sophie never invited me to join her, so even though I was kind of upset with her, I followed her to the kitchen. This was very strange. For months, Sophie

had pretty much ignored me, only talking to me to boss me around. Then again, she was being bossy *right now*. So maybe it wasn't that strange.

"Close your eyes!" Sophie yelled.

I stopped walking and closed my eyes. Yep, she was back to being bossy Sophie.

She took my arm and led me forward. I felt the kitchen table against my stomach, so we had to stop walking.

"No peeking," she said.

"I'm not!" I kept my eyes closed so tight that I saw pinpricks of light, like stars, on the backs of my eyelids.

Sophie helped me sit down. My heart did a tap dance in my chest. I didn't know what to expect.

"Okay," Sophie said. "You can open your eyes."

When I opened my eyes, I had to blink a few times because everything was blurry from squeezing my eyes so hard. On the table right in front of me was a small fish tank. One bright red fish with a flowing tail swam around in circles.

"Oh, you got a pet," I said. My shoulders slumped. Sophie got a pet before I did, after all. Maybe this was her wish. At least she'd be able to color in her daruma's other eye. I was happy for her. "It's pretty."

"No," Sophie said. "It's *your* pet. Your very own fish. I know it's not a flamingo, but this is all yours."

I glanced at Sophie to see if she was joking.

Like I said, sometimes her jokes aren't very funny. But she was smiling at me in a nice way, like she used to when we did stuff together.

"You got this for me?" I asked.

She shrugged. "I felt bad for you about your wish. I asked Dad to take me to the pet store this morning. Sorry it's not a flamingo."

I leaned my face close to the tank and the fish swam over to me.

"Wowee zowee, Sophie," I said. "I think he likes me!"

"He's a betta fish and lives alone, so you don't have to worry about him getting lonesome," Sophie said. "Make sure you read this care sheet from the pet store."

I turned to my sister and said, "Thank you." And before she could pull away, I hugged her. She hugged me back! Now I knew that even if she was bossy or ignored me sometimes,

Sophie really did like me. If only I'd wished that, then I could color in my daruma's second eye.

We watched my fish swim up and down and in circles.

"It's a bummer that you can't color in your daruma's other eye," Sophie said. "I don't think I'll ever get to color mine in either."

"Why not? What did you wish?" I asked.

Sophie sighed. "I might as well tell you, since it won't ever come true. I wished we could go to Japan and visit Obaachan," she said quietly.

I blinked at my sister. "You made a wish for all of us?"

She nodded. "But I didn't know we had to work to make our wishes come true. I have no idea how to make the trip happen."

"You can do it, Sophie! I'm sure you'll find a way. You're really smart."

"You think?" Sophie smiled at me.

"I know!" I hoped Sophie's wish would come true, not only because I wanted to go to Japan, but also because if I couldn't color in my daruma's other eye, I hoped at least she could color in hers.

FLAMINGO KEEPER

After lunch, Dad moved the little fish tank onto my desk. I decided to name my fish Daruma, since he was red like my wishing doll. It made me happy to watch him swim, and it made me really happy that Sophie had given him to me.

I finished my collage for Linnie with both Daruma and my daruma doll watching over me. I wished there were some way for me to color in the doll's other eye. I thought about what Obaachan had said about gambatte and never giving up. I didn't want to give up, but how could I get a flamingo?

The only place I'd ever seen a flamingo was at the zoo. I understood now that we couldn't have a pet flamingo at home, but what if I could get a pet flamingo and keep him at the zoo? I could go there to feed him and take care of him. I'd play fetch with him and he wouldn't ever get lonesome because he could live with the flock at the zoo! This was an excellent idea!

Mom was in the living room reading. I climbed up next to her.

"Mom? Can I use the computer? I want to look at the zoo's website," I said. I hoped I could find out if they would let you keep your pets there. And maybe they would help me find a flamingo of my own.

"Of course." Mom brought her laptop over to me and put it on the coffee table.

I clicked on the zoo's website and scrolled around. There wasn't anything about keeping your pets at the zoo. I sighed. I kept looking, and then I saw something interesting. I clicked on the link and read the first line to myself.

"Mom!" I jumped up and down. "We can adopt a flamingo! It says so right here!"

Mom leaned over to read the screen. "You're right, Jasmine. You *can* adopt a flamingo!"

"Can I? I promise to take good care of him! You could drive me to the zoo every day so I can feed him and play with him and pet him . . ." I kept hopping around the living room. I was full of happy energy.

When Mom didn't answer me right away, I stopped hopping. She was still reading the page. I walked back over to her.

"Well, Jasmine, I think this is a fine idea and you would definitely get to adopt a flamingo, but it's not quite like you imagine."

"It isn't?" I sat down next to Mom.

"You don't get to play with it or take care of it yourself. The zookeepers who are trained to take care of animals do that for you," Mom said. "You send in money and the money goes toward paying for supplies for the animal you adopt. That's a very wonderful way to help a flamingo."

"I won't get to feed it shrimpy things or pet it?" I asked, a heavy feeling settling in my chest.

"No, but remember we talked about this. Flamingos are wild animals. You're helping them by donating money. You also get a certificate of adoption with photos and a fact sheet," Mom said.

That wasn't the same as having my own flamingo, but helping a flamingo did sound nice. I could frame my certificate and flamingo photo and hang them on my wall.

"Would you like to do this?" Mom asked.

"Dad and I will be happy to pay for it. You've worked hard to show us how responsible you are."

"Yes!" I said. "My very own flamingo! Thank you, Mom!"

I watched as she filled out the form online. And once she paid, there was a message that said I'd get my certificate in the mail. I couldn't wait!

I had to wait a long time. After two weeks, my certificate and the photos of my flamingo finally arrived. *Wowee zowee!* My flamingo was beautiful! He stood tall on stilt-like legs as though he was proud of his pink feathers. On the certificate was my name, Jasmine Toguchi, beneath the words *Certificate of Adoption of a Flamingo*. I, Jasmine Toguchi, had my very own flamingo!

"You ready to go?" Dad asked me.

"One second," I said. I ran to my room. I picked up my daruma doll and squinted. I carefully colored in his other eye with my purple marker. When I was done, I put him down next to Daruma's fish tank.

"He looks good with two eyes," Sophie said from my doorway.

93

"And one day you'll get to color in yours," I said. "It feels good to make your wish come true. You can do it, Sophie!"

She smiled. "Come on. Let's go to the zoo and see your flamingo."

AUTHOR'S NOTE

The daruma (*dah-roo-mah*) is a doll made of papier-mâché that is believed to bring good luck. The daruma is a wishing doll. When a person buys or receives a daruma, he or she makes a wish or a goal, then colors in one eye. When the wish or goal is achieved, then the person colors in the other eye.

The daruma doll is based on a real person, a Buddhist monk who sat in meditation for many years. It is his perseverance that is embodied in the daruma doll. The doll is oval, without any arms or legs, and it is weighted at the bottom. If you try to tip the doll over, it stands back up. This is meant to symbolize never giving up on your wish or goal. You might get knocked down, but you get right back up and keep trying. The stern look on the doll's face shows his determination—determination to work toward making a wish or goal come true.

It is said that in the seventeenth century, the farmers in Takasaki, Japan, were suffering from hunger and poverty. The local temple had the people make daruma dolls to sell for extra income. Today, most daruma are still made in Takasaki.

Artists take recycled paper and turn it into pulp. The paper pulp is then formed into a mold of the daruma. Each doll is painted by hand. First, the daruma is rolled in the base paint (most often red) to cover the body. Once the body is dry, an artist uses a brush to paint the details of the face and body with a steady hand.

Red is the traditional color for daruma because the Buddhist monk on whom the doll is based wore a red robe. Red is also considered a lucky color. These wishing dolls come in other colors, too. Yellow is for money or fortune, orange is for success in school, and green is for good health. If you like, you can choose the color of your doll based on your wish!

DARUMA DOLL CRAFT

Make your own daruma to wish on, or to give as a gift to a friend or family member!

MATERIALS

- White paper plate
- Black and red markers
- Glue
- Gold glitter

INSTRUCTIONS

1. On one side of the paper plate, use a black marker to draw an oval on the top half of the

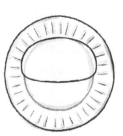

plate. This is the outline of the face of the daruma.

2. Then use the black marker to draw the eyebrows and empty circles for eyes inside the oval. Use the red marker to draw a mouth.

3. Using the red marker, color in the rest of the plate, which will be the body of the daruma.

4. Decorate his clothes by using glue to make lines or designs on the body. Sprinkle gold glitter on the glue.

5. Set aside to dry.

6. Make a wish or set a goal, then color in one eye of the daruma. When your wish or goal is achieved, color in the other eye.

Good luck and have fun!

Turn the page for a sneak peek of . . .

JASMINE TOGUCHI

MOCHi QUEEN

DEBBi MiCHiKO FLORENCE PICTURES BY ELIZABET VUKOVIĆ

Available now!

A TERRIFIC IDEA

It was safest for me to hide in my room. Mom was scrubbing the guest bathroom. Dad was getting the cardboard boxes from the garage. My big sister, Sophie, was sweeping the kitchen floor. I waited for my chance to escape the cleaning frenzy.

I, Jasmine Toguchi, do *not* like to clean! But I do like to climb trees, eat dessert, and make messes. I'd rather do any of those things right now.

I peeked out my bedroom window. Dad has moved into the backyard! I tiptoed out of my room. Nobody in the hall! I ran to the front door. But just as I put my hand on the doorknob, I heard footsteps behind me.

"Jasmine Toguchi, where do you think you're going?"

I turned slowly to face my mother.

"We need to clean the house before everyone arrives tomorrow," Mom said. "Now go help your sister."

Walnuts! This was *exactly* what I was trying to avoid. Helping Sophie would mean that I did all the work while she bossed me around.

"I already finished sweeping," Sophie announced from the next room. Scattered across the kitchen floor, small mounds of dust and bits of trash sat like sand dunes on the beach. Except this was no vacation. "You can pick it all up. I'll let you know if you do a good job."

Sophie is two years older than me. She thinks that makes her my boss. If that weren't annoying enough, she also gets to do everything before me. She started school first. She learned to read first. She even started piano lessons last year, and I have to wait another year. Not that I really want to play the piano.

Sophie was always the expert. She thought she was smarter and better than me. Just once, I wished I could do something first. Just once, I wanted to be the expert.

As I swept the piles into the dustpan, Sophie climbed up onto the kitchen stool. It was like being higher up made her more in charge. This meant barking commands at me while she picked at the chipped polish on her fingernails.

"You missed a pile!"

"Stop sweeping so hard! You're making dust fly into the air!"

"Don't spill or you'll have to clean it up."

I sighed and swept.

We were getting ready for mochi-tsuki. Every year, our relatives come over to our house to celebrate New Year's. We spend the entire day making mochi, Japanese sweet rice cakes. It's hard work to make mochi, but there's a reward—eating the gooey treat afterward.

Actually, all the other relatives do the hard work. In my family, you had to be at least ten years old to make mochi. This year would be Sophie's first time getting to help. I'm only eight. Once again, Sophie would do something before I did. By the time I was ten and got to make mochi, too, she would be the expert and boss me around. That would take all the fun out of it.

This year, just like last year, I would be stuck babysitting.

I bent over, scooped, and walked to the trash can to empty the dustpan. I did this a hundred times, at least.

I wished I could help with mochi-tsuki. I didn't want

to watch DVDs with my four-year-old cousins. It wasn't fair. I was big enough to make mochi!

"I'm going to help make mochi," I said to Sophie.

She kept picking at her orange nails. "You're too little. You'll only get in the way."

"I'm big enough." Yesterday I noticed I came up to Sophie's chin. During the summer I came up to her shoulder. I was growing!

"Just wait your turn," she said.

This year, Sophie would sit at the table in the backyard with Mom and all the other women. She would probably get to sit right next to Obaachan, our grandma who came from Japan every year for the holidays.

"Stop pouting and finish cleaning," Sophie said. "You'll get your turn at mochi-tsuki when you're ten."

I wished there was something I could do before her. Something she could never do.

I swept up another dust pile. Suddenly, I got

an idea. It was tradition for Dad, the uncles, and the boy cousins to turn the cooked rice into the sticky mochi by pounding it in a stone bowl with a big wooden hammer. That's what I could do. I could pound mochi with the boys!

"What are you grinning about?" Sophie scooted off the stool and took the dustpan from me. "Sweep the floor again to make sure there's nothing left."

You needed to be strong to pound mochi. I was strong. So I swept the floor using all my muscles.

"Stop!" Sophie screeched. "You almost hit me! Mom! Jasmine tried to whack me in the head with the broom!"

Hitting Sophie sounded like good practice for pounding mochi, but I knew it would only get me in trouble.

Just then Mom walked into the kitchen, her forehead wrinkled like it always was when she got annoyed.

"Jasmine Toguchi! You know better than that. Go clean your room if you can't work well with your sister."

I handed the broom to Sophie with a smile and skipped to my room to work on my terrific idea!

Have you joined Jasmine on all of her adventures?
Check out these other stories featuring your favorite flamingo keeper!

JASMINE TOGUCHI

MOCHI QUEEN

DEBBI MICHIKO FLORENCE PICTURES BY ELIZABET VUKOVIĆ

JASMINE TOGUCHI

SUPER SLEUTH

DEBBI MICHIKO FLORENCE PICTURES BY ELIZABET VUKOVIĆ

JASMINE TOGUCHI

DRUMMER GIRL

DEBBI MICHIKO FLORENCE PICTURES BY ELIZABET

JASMINE TOGUCHI

FLAMINGO KEEPER

DEBBI MICHIKO FLORENCE PICTURES BY ELIZABET VUKOVIĆ